Broken Silence

Black Hills Wolves
Book 42

By
Jennifer Kacey

This book is a work of fiction. Names, characters, places, and incidents are the products of the author's imagination or used fictitiously. Any resemblance to actual events, locales or persons, living or dead, is entirely coincidental.

Copyright © 2016 by Jennifer Kacey
ISBN: 978-1-61333-966-4
Cover art by Fiona Jayde

Published by Decadent Publishing Company, LLC
Look for us online at:
www.decadentpublishing.com

~A Note from Jennifer Kacey~

I NEVER thought I'd write about wolves because I'm so picky when it comes to paranormal books. They have to be impeccable, and unique, and easy to follow.

But when I was asked to write in this series, the Black Hills Wolves creators and authors that have come before me, made it impossible for me to say no.

This world, this family is incredible and I can't tell you how thrilled I am to be a part of it.

Writing keeps me sane. I love stories that are hot. It's all I read and it's certainly all I write. By the end of my stories I hope you need a cold drink, a fan, and a DO NOT DISTURB sign to hang on your door.

My wish for each of my stories is that they grab you, and stay with you as you find the next book to fall in love with. I hope my characters are real to you and you miss them when the story ends.

And above everything else I love…love. It's timeless, and classic, and filled with hope because no story is complete without a happily ever after.

I'm a traveling girl with one foot in Texas and the other in New York. These are my two favorite places to write about and they tend to wind their way throughout by books.

And I'll tell you each a secret. I ALWAYS put

something in each of my books that has happened to me. Could be something small like a gift or a glance across the room. Could be something huge as in the entire premise of a book and a what-if brought to life. What is it in this story? *grins* I'll never tell…

Jennifer Kacey
www.jenniferkacey.com/

Dedication

To Rebecca Royce – for giving me Paul. And letting me give him wings…

Acknowledgments

To Virginia Nelson – for your follicular inspiration! And to Sara. The scene with the boots? That one's for you!!

Chapter One

A bad dream.

Paul wanted it to be nothing but a bad dream.

Nothing but his subconscious vomiting something awful because bar business stressed him or he ate something bad—or maybe because he'd watched a scary movie he couldn't shake.

Too bad it wasn't anything so simple.

It wasn't a bad dream.

That couldn't have been further from the truth.

As he walked closer to the barn in his twelve-year-old body he knew what was going to happen.

He screamed at himself to stop. *Don't open the door. Turn back.*

He didn't listen.

The weathered hinges creaked as he opened the door.

The door wasn't even there anymore. The barn, burnt to the ground. He knew that, yet still couldn't shake himself away from remembering. Reliving.

It was a flashback. Not a dream. Not even a nightmare because he'd already lived every moment of it.

The smell of the barn was ripe in his nose. The wind followed him inside and swirled the dust until he had to squint.

A few random males were inside the barn. Hanging around the Alpha to get on his good side probably—if he had a good side anymore. Some days Paul wondered if he'd lost it in the bottom of one of the bottles of booze at his feet.

His Alpha, Magnum, larger than life sat off to one side at a table with his five friends. The scent of alcohol, some old and some fresh, hit his nose making it twitch. Hoping his Alpha would be in a good mood was much more than he could have hoped for, but he was only a boy.

Fairy tales and miracles still filled his head and he knew he wanted to be one of the dominant males one day.

To make a difference.

To protect the weaker pack members and the

women and children who didn't have enough to eat.

His stomach growled at the mere thought of food and his Alpha must have heard it.

"Boy. What the fuck are you doing here?"

Paul was tall for twelve, a kid not yet a man, but it was nothing compared to how big a full-grown wolf was. Throw in five more of them staring him down and he had a hard time finding his voice.

He took a deep breath and tried to calm down. He couldn't stay quiet any longer. "The pack is hungry, Alpha. Some of the older wolves are starving."

"So?"

"Uhh…." Raised to respect his Alpha, he didn't intend to be rude or anything. Surely it would do some good. Magnum had to see the good in what he was going to tell him. "Is there any way we could have some of the extra food you have stored up in the top of the barn?" Pointing over his shoulder, he looked for a few seconds to make sure it was still there.

There were boxes of extra long-term food up top he'd found a few days before looking for something

Gee the bear sent him to fetch.

"It's all right there." He turned around again and jumped back with a squeak. Magnum had moved in those scant few seconds to loom over him. Staring him down.

"What do you think you found—boy?" The larger man's head tilted to the side, and Paul had the distinct feeling he knew exactly what a bug felt like.

"F-f-food. Crackers and canned meat like…tuna…and…." Paul's throat dried up as his Alpha advanced on him. Adrenaline coursed through his veins at the growling timbre of Magnum's voice.

"If you know what's good for you, you'll forget what you saw up there and get the hell out of here."

"But there's a lot up there and—"

Pain exploded on the right side of his face and he hit the ground. Cradling his cheek, he couldn't find his voice. If he opened his mouth, he'd start screaming, so he flinched instead and ground his teeth.

"Couldn't take a hint could you, you little fucker."

His brain was muddy from the hit he'd taken and he couldn't breathe past the fear.

"Scared now aren't you?" Magnum snatched him by the back of the neck, yanking him off the floor to shake him like a rag doll.

His eye swelling shut made it hard for him to fight as Magnum dragged him across the floor toward his buddies still sitting at their table.

"I was trying to help. We're hungry. Why are you doing this? I'm sorry. I'm sorry. Please let me go. I want my mom." All of it tumbled out of him as he struggled and fought to get away.

It was supposed to go well. He was supposed to help the pack, and his parents were going to be so proud of him.

But it wasn't good.

Didn't help.

"Hold him." His Alpha threw him at the feet of his buddies. Cam, Tate, Greg, Poh, and Leo. Five men who looked like the devil himself as Paul scrambled like a crab to get away from them.

Sight all but gone in one eye, he kicked at the

man who latched onto one of his ankles. And, one by one, they immobilized him.

Chest to the ground, he continued to struggle, but he couldn't see any of them because one of the bullies had latched onto a fistful of his hair to hold him still.

He couldn't see them but he could hear them.

Each of them. As they laughed.

Laughed, as his Alpha, the man supposed to protect him and all others in the pack, brought out a vise clamp and a knife.

"Dig his tongue out, Cam."

Fingers from the man's free hand, latched onto his hair, dug in his mouth trying to get between his clenched teeth. His hand tasted like dirt and God knew what else, and Paul gagged. Cam seized the opportunity and pulled his tongue free and held it until Magnum got the clamp on it. Drool rolled down his chin and he gagged again.

He babbled but no words were discernible through his tears.

"I'm gonna silence his bratty mouth for good."

Paul tried to shake his head no but he could

barely move. Someone had to save him. There were other men in the barn. Someone had to help him. They had to. They couldn't let this happen.

"We gonna let him shift to heal?" Cam asked, yanking his hair harder.

"No," Magnum answered and Paul panicked.

"What if it kills him?" one of the other men asked. He didn't sound concerned. Merely curious.

Curious?

Paul's heart pounded away in his chest as he tried in vain to free himself, and he started to scream.

Cam yanked his head back so he was forced to face Magnum.

He smiled, the look dripping with malicious glee. "One less mouth to feed. Would serve you right for thinking you're better than us. Knowing better than us. Let's make an example out of him."

A lesson. That's what he'd called it. A lesson to everyone else in the pack who thought they needed to speak up against him.

The knife. It came closer.

In slow motion, sunlight glinted off the blade of

the dirty knife as Magnum flashed it in front of his face.

He went rigid.

The pain….

Paul woke screaming.

Well. His version of screaming. A bit different with no tongue. He tried to strangle the noise in his throat by clenching his teeth and it finally worked.

Breath rushed in and out of his lungs and he wiped at his face.

Wet.

Wet with blood.

Panic gripped him as he fumbled for the light on his nightstand.

Several things hit the floor before he found the switch.

Wiping his face again, his heart stopped as he looked at his hand.

Sweat.

His head hit the headboard as he relaxed.

It was only sweat. Thank God.

Jennifer Kacey

He counted to a hundred to try to calm his erratic pulse. And then did it again until he could breathe normally.

His future was Hail Mary'd that day. His life was thrown as hard as possible into the wind with who knew what on the other end.

He could have died. If he were human, he probably would have.

Yet—he'd lived.

Some days he wondered if surviving was a good thing or a bad thing.

Things were better with Drew, the new Alpha—an immeasurable amount better. More than a decade after he was ostracized from the pack, Drew returned to take his rightful place at the head of it. Challenging his father, Drew killed Magnum in an alpha challenge.

It was quick. Decisive.

The fact someone had been poisoning Magnum for some time played little into the outcome of the fight. Paul had his suspicions, but he *said* nothing—warned no one. Magnum's death proved far quicker

9

than Paul had wanted.

The man who mutilated him should have suffered. He didn't like having those feelings but they were there. They were there for Magnum and for the five wolves who'd stolen his future.

They were all dead—every one of them. Taken out because they couldn't be trusted. Killed because they'd decided their hate was worth fighting for.

They'd been wrong.

Sometimes….

Sometimes Paul wouldn't remember they were dead. Sometimes getting stuck in the past was as simple as slipping on an old coat full of holes. The illusion of warmth clung to his foggy brain but he was so cold. His faith in others? Fleeting, so he had a hard time putting his trust in anyone.

Or friendship.

Or love.

He shook his head and ran his fingers over his short blond hair, making sure it was still cropped close to his skull.

Short. He always kept his hair short now.

Short enough no one could grab it.

Never again would it be used against him.

Staring at his hands in front of him, he measured their width. Their size was the same as the other wolves in the pack, but his hands didn't pull the same weight. He was damaged goods. Unable to speak to anyone, he looked at the nightstand to find his only method of communicating. Two things which hadn't fallen were his notepad and pen he kept with him all the time. So he could write clipped messages to people when he had to communicate.

It got the job done, but the necessity left him even more disconnected. Relaxing his biceps, he let his hands fall to his lap then closed his eyes, as he tried to focus past the nightmare.

The pack had hope again—stronger than ever thanks to the deaths. They'd found unity and faith in their Alpha. Hell, they even found faith in each other, in their pack, first decimated by a madman then wounded by another.

The members of the Black Hills Wolves were coming home. He was happy to be a part of the growth. Happy to help welcome them back. He'd stayed for so many years with the hope of witnessing the resurrection of their pack.

Theirs.

Not his.

Never his, because he was separate from them. Lesser. He'd never be Alpha. Sure as hell wasn't a dominant wolf by any stretch of the word. Barely even a beta with the females of the pack. He was relegated to being an omega. A weakling. Yes they all told him he was needed. Wanted even. They told him omegas made the pack stronger, they helped—but how? No, he didn't see it.

He shook his head and rubbed it one more time.

The night was so silent all around him.

Where he always stayed. In the silence.

Most days it still felt as if he were free falling toward a black future with nothing to hold onto. Where he'd land, he didn't know.

All he prayed for each night and every morning? To find when he landed—he wouldn't be alone.

Chapter Two

It took Presley Ginger, whom everyone called PG, forever to track down Saja Lyons. Weeks after talking to Claudia Donovan at Columbia University, she rolled into Los Lobos to hug her up something fierce.

PG and Saja had been super close in college when they were both getting their master's degrees— sociology, the study of people. Passion for discovery and understanding was one of the many things she and Saja had in common.

They'd both started traveling their final year and lost touch. Several times over the years Presley tried to track her down, but she'd never had any luck. It struck her as a bit odd, actually—almost as if she completely disappeared. Professor Donovan used to say the same thing, but like PG—she never gave up looking. Then, when she was about to give up, which totally sucked because she really needed to talk to her, she popped up on a genealogy forum she happened to be looking at, and a phone call later confirmed for her that the Saja online was *her* Saja.

Seemed like fate and PG was a big believer in everything happening for a reason.

PG had lost her grant after her thesis was completed. Kinky sex was no longer relevant, she was told, more than once, and she put the steering wheel in a bit of a choke hold.

"Not relevant my ass," she mumbled under her breath.

She needed Saja's help on the next adventure she had in mind so she'd be back on track to save the world. Well, at least her little piece of it.

It was odd, though. At first when she'd asked where she lived—or at least worked—so she could visit her, Saja had refused, which wasn't like her at all.

Then PG had asked if Saja could come see her, which was met with another no.

And not a no as in, not this week, it was more like a no as in never.

Then, a few days later, Saja'd called her cell

completely excited and told her to come on and not to dilly dally on her way to Rapid City. Something about the full moon was in there, but she lost her on the last part.

Sounded as if she'd had to move heaven and earth and a few dead presidents to allow her to come.

She was thankful. Couldn't wait to see her long lost friend so she followed the instructions to the letter. In Rapid City, a man named Jasper would pick her up and give her a ride. The picture Saja texted her helped her identify her temporary chauffeur, and the man proved a genial companion.

Still, it was hard not to be a bit head scratchy about the whiplash kind of turnaround she'd dealt her. The drive took a while, and she lost track of the number of switchbacks Jasper took. When they turned down a bouncy track, she leaned forward. Saja had said the location was remote—not third world.

'Cause, damn.

Rolling her window down at the edge of Los Lobos, she studied the recovering town. New establishments interspersed older, more worn shops.

The presence of new wood amongst the old said a lot for local revitalization.

As Jasper crawled down the street, she noticed how many people were outside. Seemed like any other small town she'd been through. Everyone stared. Rainbow hair tended to get attention. Only a handful amongst the crowd seemed to wear jackets even though it was a little chilly out. She shivered, but she was always cold anyway.

The building Jasper parked in front of was bigger—and nicer than she expected.

Odd though because this wasn't some overly decorated place with lights and hoopla. Simply a sign which read *The Den*—and a very crowded parking lot.

Something to be said about the place. It attracted a large crowd with nothing fancy. Maybe the food was all amazing, home cooked, and featured on one of those cooking shows like diners and dives or something.

When he parked, she got out and stretched. "Thanks for the ride, Jasper. Not gonna say it hasn't been a bit weird needing an escort, but I appreciate you bringing me here."

He nodded and drove off.

Maybe it was her new deodorant.

She smiled, threw her phone in her purse, and headed in.

Inside it wasn't so much dark as it was much less bright than outside, and it took her eyes a minute to adjust.

Didn't take half the same time for a hush to fall over the rather crowded space.

Glancing around lifted her smile and spirits when she spotted Saja. She stood at the bar next to some jacked-up, maybe Native American, dude. Looked like she was sweet-talking him into something and he was doing a whole lotta shrugging.

In the middle of a sentence, Saja turned and squealing times two filled the place.

"You're here," Saja laughed as they hugged.

"I missed you," PG admitted as she held onto her friend. "It's been way too long."

Hugging lasted for a while until Saja dragged her over and plunked her down in the middle of the crowded restaurant.

PG put her purse on an open chair and looked at the table. "Menus?"

"Not needed."

"What do you mean? I've never eaten here before. I have no idea what they have."

"I can cover it on three fingers."

PG gave her the squirrely eye and Saja held up one finger at a time.

"Fried pickles, a hamburger, and broccoli. Sometimes with cheese. Sometimes not."

"You're joking."

"Nope."

There went her dreams of a food show showing up with TV cameras.

"How odd. Did the place open recently?"

"Nope, it's been open for decades. Same menu."

"And people keep coming back?"

Saja looked around proudly to the busy place. "In droves." Her smile lit the entire bar and she took PG's hand and gave it a squeeze.

Someone walked up to their table and put a bowl

of fried pickles in the center.

PG looked up, and up. Holy tall and sexy.

Blond. Broad. Gorgeous.

Must have been the waiter and she forgot the simple menu.

Saja spoke up. Thankfully, she remembered how to speak. "Hey, Paul. Can we have a diet soda for PG and water for me—or maybe some tea if Gee made it?"

He glanced in PG's general direction and she smiled so big she almost giggled. Holy shit, as if she'd never seen a hot guy before. She normally had a better game than crazy teenager.

Still, he never met her eyes. Turning away, he retreated toward the bar.

"Thank you," PG called after him hoping to get a smile or a wink or a something.

Still nothing. No turn around. Or wave over the shoulder. Nothing.

"Uhh? What was that about?"

"What?" Saja looked completely clueless.

PG pointed toward Mr. Hot and Silent as he

lifted the panel to get behind the bar. "He didn't even look in my direction. And he was so quiet. Didn't say a word to either of us. And he looked so sad."

Her friend seemed to stop and measure her words. "He's mute actually."

"Uhh…." Totally the last thing she'd expected her to say. "Why?"

"Years ago there was a bit of an—accident—and he lost the ability to speak. Been mute ever since."

There were so many holes in the story she figured she could have walked through them. She watched Paul as he got an entire tray of drinks ready, and decided the whys of it truly didn't matter.

"He can hear me though?"

"Perfectly."

Excitement nearly burst from inside her. "Great! I'm going to go talk to him." PG was up and out of her seat in half a second.

Saja's string of "buts" echoed behind her as she took each step.

"It's all good. Promise," she stage whispered from behind her hand and back over her shoulder.

More people, men and women, stared at her. Though she totally wanted to tell them to take a picture, she worried they might. Odd but the vibe in the bar was sort of electric. She'd never felt anything like it before. It increased the closer she got to the sexy man behind the counter, too.

And the rest of the patrons of the bar seemed like they were waiting for something. All of them were a bit antsy. As if a big event were about to happen. Might have something to do with why Saja was hesitant to let her come.

Maybe they had a town festival or something.

She shrugged to herself and cut them all some slack. Everyone was entitled to have a bad day.

Before she lost her nerve, she knelt on a barstool. Leaning over, she tapped the hot waiter on the shoulder. "Excuse me?" The question came out breathy and heat raced up her spine.

The touch wasn't necessary.

Well it wasn't needed to get his attention but it felt vitally important to her for some reason. Having such a visceral reaction to a man hadn't even really happened to her.

The longing was nothing compared to what happened to her insides when he turned around and looked at her.

Fuck. Talk about hot.

He was definitely tall, with close-cropped light-blond hair and a tan begging to be licked. Gorgeous light-blue eyes completed his beautiful package, and they reminded her of a cloudless sky.

Hi. She signed it to him and he blinked several times.

Signing to him was as natural as breathing. He had to have a way to communicate and sign language made the most sense to her. *I'm Presley but my friends call me PG. Nice to meet you.*

He hesitated. Stared at her. Seemed like forever. Then he tentatively signed back. *I'm Paul. You sign.*

She couldn't tell if the last two words were a question or a statement so she kind of winged it from there. *Yes. I minored in sign language for my bachelor's degree. Have been an interpreter off and on for years.*

A what? Can you say it and give me the sign for it again? Those aren't ones I've seen before.

"Interpreter." She said it, spelled it out, and then gave him the sign for it again.

He signed it back several times, and the last couple were perfect.

You got it.

Who have you signed for?

Lots of people actually. Several foreign dignitaries coming into the university I attended. A couple people on grant panels I've needed it for. Churches always seem to need someone. You'd be surprised how many people need an interpreter.

Is that why you started? To have a job skill?

For someone who had been mute for a long time, his signing was a bit reserved. *Oh. No. My grandmother was deaf so I started signing when I was little so I could talk to her. Have always loved having it. Has come in handy several times. Such as today.*

He closed his eyes for a second as if composing himself or saying a prayer. Then he nodded toward her. *Can't tell you how glad I am you are here today.*

23

Well didn't he just make her feel all giddy inside, but she tried to be cool and not drool on the bar.

For several minutes, they chatted back and forth, and then PG slowed down when some random guy sat down next to her, watching the interaction with open interest. Totally odd and a bit rude, but she didn't let it stop her.

Then she paused altogether.

The silence in the room seemed deafening. Seriously. No one else was talking, eating, walking, moving. Nothing. A standstill would have been hoofing it faster. And every gaze in the place was on them. Riveted.

You'd think none of them have ever seen you sign before. Weird.

They haven't.

"Uhh. What?"

He shook his head. *I'm out of time and it's quite a story. Not a quick one. Have to get orders out.* He motioned toward the tray of drinks she'd waylaid him from delivering earlier. *I'm going to be here for a few more hours. You going to be here when I get off?*

24

Unfortunately not. Disappointment clung to her, too, more in an ache in her gut kind of upset at not seeing him later. "Saja said I could only stay for…." She looked at her watch to calculate the time she had left and she already knew it wasn't a lot.

Mr. Up in Their Business next to them didn't let her finish checking the time. "She'll be here when you get off, Paul."

Something passed between the two men. Paul nodded, signed to her, *Bye for now*, she did the same with a big ole smile, extremely excited to see him later, and then he carried the tray around to deliver drinks.

So hot.

Turning to the guy next to her to see why he'd been so rude, the rebuke died in her throat when his smile could have powered a first world nation.

"I'm sorry I butted into your conversation, but when I walked in and he was talking to you, I was— moved. I answered for you without knowing your plans. All social cues out the window obviously. My apologies—you are welcome to stay." He still seemed a tad surprised, but in the best way possible so instead of riding his ass she held out a hand.

"Hi, I'm PG."

With a firm grip, he took her hand and pumped it a couple times as he openly studied her. "Drew." After he let her hand go, he looked around the bar, and she followed his attention.

Everyone was going about their business again, which totally meant they were trying super hard to act as if they weren't trying to listen in on every word, but they were.

"Saja's friend?" he asked.

"Yes, from school. We lost touch and I was super excited to get to come see her. Drive was beautiful. Can't believe how much I like it up here toward the mountains." Yes, she was making small talk. Might have had something to do with wanting to wait for Paul to return from the back.

Which was totally pathetic.

And totally true.

"Nice to meet you," Drew offered with a nod. "She's told us a lot about you." Then he sniffed the air. Like. Sniffed it.

Uhh....

She almost giggled and blurted out she'd tried a new deodorant that morning but decided he needed to butt into at least two more conversations before he was privy to such personal info.

Sliding off the barstool, she excused herself. "Nice to meet you." All eyes seemed to track her movements.

Everyone seemed so edgy.

Rolling her eyes, she remembered her grandmother's superstition about the crazies coming out on the full moon.

She stared around the bar as she headed back to Saja's table. The people in the place definitely seemed to fit the superstition well.

Shaking off the odd feeling was nearly as quick as her frantic heart was beating.

It felt like a magical moment right before she stepped onto the precipice of something incredible, and it was barely over the next hill and she couldn't wait to get there.

Glancing over her shoulder, she waited. He walked out of the kitchen, and Saja smiled. Because his gaze tracked to PG immediately.

Coming to talk to Saja about everything she was up to had seemed like an incredible way to check on her friend and see if she had any additional ideas on how to resurrect her academic career. Snagging more deets on the tall drink of water behind the bar was going to be the best icing on her cake for like…ever.

She stared at him as she sat down and he brought out the—broccoli.

With cheese.

Yes!

Day was looking way up already.

Chapter Three

Oddest lunch ever, but she really enjoyed it because it sure wasn't dull.

Might have had something to do with the man waiting on them.

When he'd come back to their table to check on them, and to bring their food, he'd locked eyes with her. Didn't look away until he had to. And she'd made sure and signed to him.

A simple thank you. Or to ask for ketchup.

Each time he'd answered her, his signing somewhat halting, but he spoke to her. From the hushed silence accompanying it, she actually believed him. He'd never signed to any of them before.

Hadn't even attempted it.

She shook her head and tried not to think of how isolated he must have felt.

The food was surprisingly good. Fried pickles were great. Saja kept giving her the squirrely eye every time she ate one. PG asked her several times during the meal if she was okay, and she answered "perfect" every time. Made her wonder if they were *special* pickles. Like *special* brownies.

She smiled behind her hand and decided again what a good idea it was she decided to stretch her legs a bit. All work and no play could make a girl twitchy.

As she finished the last bite of her burger, she wiped her mouth. "Saja, I didn't think I'd be so impressed with the food but I liked it."

"Told you it was good. Gee can cook a mean burger."

Saja was awesome, almost exactly how she remembered her—vivacious, friendly, open, and caring. Totally a good egg.

What was strange though?

There was this strange vibe all around them as they caught up. Never lessened the longer they sat there.

A little from Saja herself but a lot from the people eating around them gave her an odd feeling. They definitely seemed on edge, and it made her antsy like in a night-before-Christmas kind of way.

As if something epic sat on the horizon and she couldn't wait to get there.

"Who was the woman who stopped by earlier? Right before our burgers arrived." She'd been looking for Paul to come out from the back, but when Saja didn't answer, she turned around. PG smiled as Saja was chewing a huge bite. "Sorry, didn't mean to catch you mid bite."

Ryker, Saja's brooding husband, walked over from where he'd been talking to another group of people, sat down next to Saja, and rubbed her shoulders. "Tasha."

"Tasha, yes. Totally her."

How he'd heard her from across the noisy bar she didn't know, but somehow she wasn't surprised. A quiet respect surrounded him, but he sure didn't miss a thing, and people seemed to defer to him if he were around.

Several other people had come up to talk to Saja or Ryker if he was sitting with them and they'd all introduced themselves to her. Friendly yes, but it had also reminded her of being an animal at a zoo.

As if they wanted to get a look at her. Odd.

Most memorable was the lovely woman by the name of Tasha. Horrible scars ran down her face. Another accident, Saja had told her. Interesting. PG wondered how many of those happened around the Black Hills.

The other guy, Drew, got up from his barstool and made his way to their table with a slight limp.

Another accident? Hmmm....

PG liked solving puzzles and all of the people in the bar seemed to be one giant puzzle waiting for her to piece together.

Drew approached the table and Ryker stood.

Drew.

The dude wielded some kind of power. Like the mayor or something. He'd talked to probably everyone in the bar twice already. Mayor was wrong, though. Not like a politician. Something else. Sheriff, maybe?

She filed away a few more details as he sat down.

"How was your lunch?" he asked her as he nodded at her empty plate.

"Really good. Seems I was lucky since it was a cheese day."

He smiled. "Lucky, indeed. So what brings you to the Black Hills and our sleepy little town?"

"I don't think your town is sleepy. I know I haven't been here long, but it seems vibrant. Like a family reunion almost. You all seem to know each other. It's endearing, actually."

"Can't tell you how nice it is to hear. So what about you? How did you and Saja meet? She said something about school."

"Yep, we were in the same undergrad program and then the master's program."

Saja continued. "We helped each other with grant proposals, too. Mainly, PG helped me."

"Completely not true.'"

Saja kept going with a roll of her eyes. "Very true. You're a whiz with grant applications."

"Too bad I can't make a career out of it though. Which is actually why I'm here slobbering all over your hospitality. When my last grant ran out, they wouldn't fund me anymore."

33

"Why not?" Saja asked. PG glanced at the two men, expecting them to be bored stiff. Talk about couldn't have been farther from the truth. Both were locked onto the conversation and what her answer would be. "Said they didn't feel the research would be beneficial enough on a global scale. Asshats. They couldn't see my vision and didn't want to try. It was like they were scared of what I'd find."

"Which was?" Ryker prompted.

Paul walked out from the back and sought her immediately with his gaze. Hiding her delight at seeing him didn't happen and her smile took over. Didn't take long for him to have to go back into the kitchen, but his presence made her happy. She blinked at the other three people at her table and completely forgot what they were talking about. "Sorry. What was the question?"

Saja didn't even try to cover up her laugh. "I don't think I've ever seen you so distracted. It's charming. And we'll get back to the grant stuff in a second. I didn't realize you still signed. Completely fortuitous."

A notion flitted through PG's head. "Did you bring me here because I signed? To talk to Paul?"

"I wish I'd been anywhere close to that smart because I would have been a complete rock star, but none of us knew he was learning ASL on his own. Knowing you signed wouldn't have crossed my mind as something able to benefit him. Sounding more and more like fate you came to see me."

"Fate, huh?"

Saja looked at Ryker and then back. "Maybe more than we thought possible. I'm starting to think she answers prayers." PG opened her mouth to ask something about what she'd said but Saja continued. "Still signing for your grandmother?"

"No. She passed a few years ago. Suddenly. Don't know which is worse, you know? When someone you love dies, is it better to know it's coming so you can prepare or for it to happen out of nowhere?"

"Oh, honey. I'm so sorry." Her friend reached over and gave her hand a squeeze. "I know how close you were to her."

"Very. My parents and I never really had anything in common," she added for the benefit of the two men sitting with them. "My grandmother was my rock. Miss her like crazy. She was my roots. My home base. That's better. No matter where I was traveling I always knew I had a place to come home. Miss her tons."

"What about her house? Not like your parents needed another place."

"They sold it."

"What? Why?"

PG scrunched up her mouth and eyebrows and tried her best to imitate her father. "You aren't responsible enough to maintain our kind of estate, Presley. Maybe once you grow up and get a real job you can—"

"Stop there." It was Drew who spoke and shook his head. "I know something about asshole fathers. Sometimes you have to go your own way."

"Amen. And you know what? They don't break us, right?" She waggled her eyebrows at Drew.

He chuckled. "They most certainly don't."

Jennifer Kacey

PG took a drink and shrugged. "I haven't used nor wanted their money since I turned eighteen and left the house. Amazing how much easier I could breathe when I was no longer under the roof he kept preaching about. So I've done a lot of traveling. Mostly for research, which was kink related."

Saja leaned forward. "Uh…. Kink related. Come again?"

"That's what she said."

Even Saja's stern-faced Ryker cracked a smile at her comment.

"I was researching the psychological healing kink can bring about. It was incredibly focused on adults with traumatic and—or abusive backgrounds."

"Really?" Saja's academic interest flared in her eyes, and she folded her arms as she leaned forward. "Talk about fascinating. And they pulled your funding. Why?"

"The whole fifty shades phenomenon is how I pitched it. The quote unquote normal women were reading it and loving it. How a kink book had gone so far to push the boundaries of something previously

37

considered so taboo, but sex and kink and giving up control were being talked about openly. If kink could accomplish so much for everyday housewives, then what could it do for other triggers hidden inside people?"

"What made you think of it?" Exactly why she wanted to bring the subject to Saja. Her old friend knew how to examine the angles.

"Some of our friends in college were really into it. Two of them were deaf and I used to hang out with them all the time after my other partner in crime took off for lands unknown." She looked pointedly at Saja, who smiled and looked at Ryker. "Got talking to one of them and her husband one night about it. She'd had an abusive childhood and kink was another way she could express herself without being able to hear."

Tapping two fingers against her arm, Saja nodded. "Go on."

"Interesting, right?"

"Totally."

"She couldn't hear but she could still see. The connection she and her husband built involved him

38

giving up his control to her, which was something—"

"Him?" This time it was Ryker who interrupted.

"Yes. She took control in the bedroom or the dungeon, or wherever they were at when they decided to get frisky. Her taking control, taking her power back. It was incredible."

"You saw it?" Saja whispered the words and looked as if she was about to slip out of her chair.

"Several times. Research you know."

"Huh."

"And I got close to a lot of the other Dommes she was friends with, too. Hearing their stories and why they were into kink. It was fascinating. I really thought something was there so I went after a grant."

"And won it." Ryker again.

She nodded. "A two-year grant. I went all over the world, speaking to some of the most amazing people. Most were completely open about what they did and what they were into. Some of them could tell me why. Others were simply starting out. Getting to see them grow and change and flourish in their new world. So cool."

"Then what happened? When the funding ran out, why stop? It sounds like you really had something there." Saja's brows dipped low in obvious disbelief.

PG understood the feeling. "When the fifty shades movie came out and it was under so much scrutiny and controversy, they decided they didn't want to fund something with the potential to blow up in their faces."

"Yet it could also have been something amazing that could blow the mental health world on its ass."

"My feelings exactly. What I learned in two years was insane. Personally and academically, but they weren't willing to back it again. Disappointing, but I decided to see it as my cue to take a breather and figure out what I wanted to do. I love people. Helping them find themselves and be happy. Truly happy. It's incredible. So now I decide if I want to go after another grant and try again, or…."

"Or?" Drew prompted.

"Or something else I guess. I feel like there's something out there waiting for me. Like it's under a rock and I have to—lift it."

Paul approached the table and butterflies bounced about in her stomach. *Can you ask Saja if she wants anything else?*

Sure. "He wanted to know if you wanted anything else." She glanced at Saja who tried to hide the huge smile on her face.

Facing Paul, Saja patted her tummy. "Stuffed. But…."

Paul raised his eyebrows, clearly in question.

"Could I have one of Gee's special burgers to go? Might be hungry later."

He started signing.

"He says coming right up."

"Awesome."

A little bit longer, okay?

Take your time. I'm not going anywhere.

Good. He turned back around to clear some tables.

"Gee spoils you." The softness in Ryker's terse tone accompanied a gentle tug of Saja's hair.

"And whose fault would that be?" She leaned

into his touch.

Drew spoke and pulled her attention away from the other couple. "Where'd you learn to write grants? I'd wondered about doing something like this for the town with the Black Hills being protected. Figured there could be some extra funds to build the town back up with. Or is the kind of grant you were going after different than the kind I would need to fill out?"

PG shrugged. "Learned it. Just takes practice. It's not crazy hard as long as you learn the formula behind it. And a grant is a grant is a grant. The end result is the same."

"Don't believe her." Saja shook her head. "There is no formula. She's like the grant whisperer."

"Well. Before you leave town, I'd really like to talk to you about it. Definitely think it could be beneficial."

They asked a lot of questions, small talk stuff mostly, but all three of them paid rapt attention to her answers. Not rude or prying. Thorough, maybe? Almost as if she were on a job interview.

Rolling her eyes, PG took another drink.

Way too many grant meetings in her recent past, apparently.

Paul strolled past with a tray of fried pickles. Saja paled then nearly knocked over her chair in her rush to dart to the bathroom.

"Saja. Saja!" PG was up and out of her seat before the door had even closed behind her friend. As soon as she walked in, the sounds of retching greeted her. She waited for Saja to pause before asking, "You okay in there? Need someone to hold your hair?"

A weak laugh filtered out of the stall, followed by a flush and the door opening.

"You look the same shade as the fried pickles."

"Ugh." She washed her face, rinsed out her mouth. "I always heard pregnant women were supposed to glow."

"Wait. Pregnant? Like…. Pregnant?"

Saja dried her face and nodded with a smile.

PG gathered her in a gentle hug. "Congratulations!"

"It's why I couldn't come see you. Can't travel right now. Tend to get car sick. Imagine that."

"It's so wonderful. Well not the car sick part of course. You're gonna be a mom."

"I know. I'm so excited. Not about the puking part though. Talk about suck."

"I hear ya."

Saja pushed out of the bathroom and Ryker met her right outside the door. "You okay?" He scooped her into his arms and held her close. Forehead to forehead.

Tears misted PG's eyes and she walked around them, deciding to give them a private moment. What a beautiful couple they made. A pang of wistfulness hit her at the concern on Ryker's face. The way he held Saja, protected her. Beautiful didn't even come close to what they had.

She tried to shake off the creeping loneliness, her constant companion since her grandmother died.

The bar had emptied out. No clue if it happened while they were talking or when Saja and she were in the bathroom. Looked like a ghost town when it was their lone table full.

Back at their four top, a beautiful redhead

perched on Drew's lap. She held out her hand as PG approached. "Hi, I'm Betty."

PG shook her hand and sat back down. "Presley, but everyone calls me PG."

"So nice to meet you. I've heard a lot about you."

"Nice to meet you, too." PG looked around and raised her eyebrows. "Where'd everybody run off to? Doesn't Gee serve dinner around here? Swear I showered."

"He normally closes early a few days of the month," Drew told her.

"Oh. How cool." She wondered if it had anything to do with Paul wanting to leave to talk to her, and the idea made her more than a little happy.

Ryker walked over with Saja and continued to hold her as if she weighed nothing. "I can walk you know."

"I know." He didn't put her down, though, and PG flushed at how intense Ryker looked at her friend.

The door to the bar opened and a man walked in. Tasha was right behind him and it wasn't as bright out anymore. They must have all been talking for a heck of a lot longer than she thought. "Drew, can I have a minute?" The newcomer stopped a few feet inside and held Tasha close.

Betty stood, as did Drew, and he took her hand. "Excuse us." They walked over to the others at the door. He and Betty were definitely a thing. Gorgeous couple.

"Everyone looks amazing here."

"What do you mean?" Saja asked, and despite her earlier protestation, she rested her head against Ryker's shoulder—seemingly content.

"Healthy. Vibrant. I'm not certain the phrase, but everyone around here looks like they're in the best shape ever. Must be something in the water."

"Or the fried pickles." Saja made a face.

"Or the fried pickles. Who knows what rejuvenating characteristics they have? Someone should get a grant to see."

They laughed as Ryker sat with Saja in his lap and faced PG. "Where did you learn to sign?"

"I learned a lot from my grandmother, actually, so I could talk to her. She taught me a huge amount

46

over the years when I was little. Learned a lot in school, too, but a lot of it was from her. There are several different kinds of sign language and I specifically focused on ASL. It's served me well."

"Could I learn?" Ryker was incredibly serious.

"Of course. Simply takes practice. Look at Paul. Sounds as if he didn't learn from someone. The Internet. Videos. Amazing what technology can do these days."

"Easier from a teacher, I'm assuming."

"Without a doubt." PG almost volunteered to be their teacher, but she wasn't staying. The thought of leaving left her feeling more adrift than she cared to admit.

Paul came out of the back with a hugemongous bear of a guy. Not a word, but if it was, there'd be a picture of him next to it in the dictionary.

"Who's he?"

Saja twisted to look, but Ryker didn't glance in their direction before answering. "Gee."

Fuck. He was huge and kept getting bigger as he approached the table.

"You PG?"

"Uh huh." Totally all she got out.

Then, out of the blue, he said, "You need a place to stay." Not a question. "I've got a free room above the bar."

"Oh." She stuffed down the *holy shit you're big* she wanted to say and found her adult button. "I'd kind of wondered what I was going to do. I'd planned on getting a ride back to Rapid City to find a room since Saja was so specific on how long I could stay." Glancing at her watch told her that time had elapsed almost two hours before.

"Can she stay?" Saja asked Ryker. "We could catch up some more and have breakfast tomorrow, and Drew could pick her brain on grant stuff. Win win, don't you think?" She batted her eyes at him.

"She can stay, but you know the rules."

But PG didn't, and she was totally confused as to why she would need permission to stay if it wasn't Ryker's room she would be staying in. So odd and her interest was totally piqued. Especially as the other two couples joined them, and she glanced at Paul again, and he hadn't taken his gaze from her since he'd walked up.

The blue color was gorgeous. Light, and filled with something she couldn't quite put her finger on.

"PG?" Saja called her.

Pulling her gaze from Paul, she looked at her. "Uh. Sorry. What?"

"I think you should stay overnight. Work for you?"

She glanced at Paul again. "Very much so."

Ryker spoke to Paul as if she couldn't hear him. "Keep her in town and don't go into the woods tonight. Got it?"

Paul finally looked at Ryker and nodded once. His gaze returned to her and he raised his hands. *You ready?*

Where we going?

Anywhere but here.

Deal. She laughed and stood.

"What did he say?" Ryker, the quiet one, asked. Despite his reserve, he must care about Paul if he wanted to know and communicate.

"He wanted to show me around town."

Ryker nodded and Paul tapped her on the shoulder.

That's not what I said.

Course not. It's one of the nicest things about signing. Hiding in plain sight.

I don't follow.

As long as you have this look on your face. She adopted a thoughtful expression and nodded as if she were considering the problem of world peace or the financial viability of some third world nation. *We could be talking about anything. The migration of barn swallows in East Texas, the mating patterns of muskrats in Indonesia, or Beavis and Butthead. They don't know any different.*

Paul laughed with his entire body. He clutched at his shirt covering his abdomen, his shoulders moved, and his teeth were gorgeous as he chuckled and shook his head.

Someone in the group behind her said, "Oh my fuck, he just laughed. Did you guys see it, too? Tell me I'm not dreaming?"

"I saw it. Swear we need to write it down somewhere. Archives are somewhere. Damn."

Paul seemed to think about going back to the somber expression it seemed he was quite used to wearing, but she touched his hand to get his attention.

Don't put it away yet.

His eyebrows went down. *What?*

Your smile. It's even better than I imagined it to be.

He hesitantly reached for her, and then paused.

Moving half a step closer, she erased the distance between them.

He moved a few strands of hair off her cheek and awareness sang through her as he smiled down at her again. Stepping even closer, her heart went pitter pat and something electric sizzled between them as she stared up at him.

Thinking she needed to say something to him, she lifted her hands but her mind was surprisingly quiet. Her fingers curled into his shirt and he pulled her closer. The warmth of his hands on her back through her shirt—no—beneath her shirt on the flesh of her spine, made her shiver.

The moment hung in the air between them and the world disappeared.

Until Gee broke the tension. "No sex in the bar. Go outside."

A little growl came out of Paul as his top lip lifted in a slight snarl. PG's pussy clenched on nothing. *Do you feel something?*

Feel what? Paul asked her. He took a deep breath and closed his eyes for a moment.

It's like electricity or power. I've never felt it before.

Me either. Let's get out of here. I don't want to be around—anyone else right now.

He stepped back and she grabbed her phone and keys off the table. "We're going for a stroll. Don't wait up."

Paul chuckled.

"I'll be damned. He laughed again." Drew shook his head, the note of wonder revealing more than anything else. Paul didn't laugh often. She wanted to change the notion.

Outside, as the sun set, they chatted, and he told her about local history, the origin of the hills, and the founders of the town. How they ran it down until it was almost a ghost town until some of the current residents banded together to make it awesome again.

He showed her some of the new businesses—a dress shop, a gardening center, another restaurant.

His excitement was palpable and even his hands shook with how fast he was trying to sign. About the town in general but also having someone to talk to about it.

His enthusiasm was infectious and she began to build a picture of the vision he presented. They wanted to restore their town. Saja helped by tracking down previous inhabitants because they'd inherited houses there or something. PG was a bit lost on that part, but she figured she'd hit Saja up at breakfast the next morning on the specifics.

The moon came out as he was showing her a lot of buildings they'd been remodeling.

"How pretty." Pointing to the full moon, she

steadied herself on Paul's arm. Electricity jolted up her bones into her chest and he yanked his arm away.

"You felt it, too. I felt something before but it's even stronger now. Outside."

He rubbed his skin, telling her he clearly felt it, too, but he didn't answer her. Then he looked at her then up at the moon. Back at her.

"Paul, are you okay?"

Backing away from her, he shook his head.

Swear to gawd his eyes changed. Not as in got all dreamy, but changed into something else for a second. Slanted. Sharper. Fierce.

She swallowed as she took a few steps closer to him. "What's wrong? What's going on?"

He shook his head and balled his hands into fists as she almost reached him.

Turning, he tried to sprint away, but with a yell he went down. She shrieked and reached for him but she missed. Not because she wasn't close enough, but because he never hit the ground.

She blinked. One blink and he was gone.

Paul no longer stood there.

What stood in his place?

A wolf with a bright silver coat.

On all fours, he stood there, faced away from her, panting.

"Paul?" Nothing but the tiniest whisper of air left her mouth.

His ears perked up, and his huge muzzle swung around, locking eyes with her. Something happened, changed, ignited inside her like a birth of a planet or an idea which was going to change the world.

In the next breath, he was gone, took off at some kind of unholy pace not even possible for a wolf much less a man.

Then his howl ripped through the night.

Holy.

Shit.

Chapter Four

Late the next morning, with his hands shoved in the pockets of his jeans and his eyes firmly on the ground, Paul walked to Gee's.

Dejected.

Lost.

Hopeless.

He'd only thought he knew what lonely felt like before yesterday. Before meeting Presley.

Presley.

Simply thinking her name sent tendrils of need racing through his veins.

To stand in the presence of everything he'd ever wanted and to have it ripped away from him was the biggest injustice he'd ever experienced.

And to have it be his fault?

He scowled harder as the bar came into view.

People said hi and he had nothing for them.

He'd majorly fucked up.

He stood a bit taller. It was his fault. Blaming

someone else wasn't going to fix it for him this time. There were no excuses for what he'd done. At least he didn't feel like an impotent hanger-on this time. At least he didn't have to swallow being someone else's responsibility this time.

This time, he could own it.

And suffer the repercussions.

Not the way he wanted to go out though. Not the way he ever saw his exit strategy from this life happening.

Going into work, he planned to leave Gee a message. Finding Drew or Ryker was the first thing he had to do. Owning he shifted, in front of his girl.... Not his girl.

Not.

His.

Girl.

He'd made sure of it after losing control of his shift.

It being the first time ever he hadn't been able to control it made no difference. Not to him. Not to his Alpha or Enforcer. And not to the pack.

Their pack. Still didn't feel like his. Though, for a short time the night before, he'd felt a part of them. A kinship he'd never thought he had the right to experience.

Yet he'd tasted it for the briefest of hours as Presley waited for him to get off work.

Her eyes when she'd seen him. Every time he'd come out of the back, she'd been watching for him.

Every time.

Fuck.

He shook his head.

A human. He'd shifted in front of a human.

They'd all been told, by Ryker, there would be no talk of wolves in front of Saja's friend. Nothing about nonhumans, or the moon, or shifting, or anything else which might disrupt the human façade they wore so they could fade into the world's background.

Or else.

It was the *or else* he was worried about.

Presley had to be long gone. Probably left tire tracks on the main drag on the way out of town.

Grinding his teeth at the thought of her gone didn't help dissipate the ache at her absence.

He'd lost control.

Never once since he came into his wolf had he been moon dependent. Not once, and he had to lose his shit in front of one of the people he *had* to keep in the dark. The fact it caught him completely off guard was no excuse, and now he had to suffer the consequences.

He'd always heard mating could fuck with his shift but—mating? Really? In an instant. Did it really happen like that?

Not to him.

It couldn't.

He wasn't that lucky.

Walking into the bar, he froze, holding the door wide open.

Her scent hit his system as if it were a drug. Sucking in another lungful, he had to fight to stay on his feet.

There she sat. Presley. His Presley, talking with Gee.

She talked. He listened.

Paul growled and she jumped, nearly falling off her stool.

Blinking at him, it didn't take her half a second to scramble the rest of the way off. He expected her to run out the back or hide behind the were-bear or scream about monsters and keel over.

Or shoot him.

Or slap him.

Instead, she ran directly at him, and he let the door go and opened his arms to her. She jumped and he caught her. The impact at her touch?

Staggered.

They went together as if they were magnets.

Her chest against his, her arms tight around his neck, her legs around his waist.

Fuck.

His eyes stung at the rightness filling him up.

He tucked her into the corner of the wall, shielding her from the rest of the world with his body.

His to protect.

She was.

Feeling her against his body, inhaling her worried scent from the side of her throat, he—

Worried.

He took another breath.

Not afraid.

"Are you okay?" she whispered.

All he could do was nod against her shoulder because letting her go to sign at her wasn't really on his schedule at the moment. Letting her go wasn't an option. He never wanted to let her go.

"No one will talk to me."

He shook his head, knowing no one could.

Gee's voice brought him up to the surface even though he would have happily drowned in her and died a happy wolf. "Find Drew or Ryker."

Last thing he wanted to do was put his girl down. And she was his. The moment he saw her again he knew he'd never willingly let her go.

What he faced with his Alpha or the Enforcer was gonna suck, but, for her, he'd do anything. Only he wasn't willing to lie down and take whatever punishment they thought appropriate. Death wasn't

61

an option anymore. Life without her was a worse kind of death he wouldn't survive.

Fixing it was the only option or he'd flee with her. Live somewhere else.

They'd make it work. They had to.

He let her slide down his body, and they separated enough for him to pull her back over to the barstools and sloppily sign at her. *I can't talk to you yet. Have to go talk to someone else first. I can't mess up again if I still have any chance of fixing this.*

"But why can't you tell me—"

In walked Saja and Ryker. Looking at them, Paul pulled Presley into his side with a glare.

By the cast of Ryker's eyes to the shift in position, the move wasn't lost on the Enforcer. "We need to talk."

How he knew didn't really make much difference. And if Gee knew what happened, which he clearly did by the sympathetic look he cast him, then Ryker and Drew knew as well.

"I want to go, too. I can interpret. I can—"

Paul covered Presley's lips with his fingers and

shook his head. *You can't. It's not the way here. I'll talk to you afterward. Tell you everything.*

She stared up at him with wet eyes. *Promise?*

A tear slid free and he wiped it away. *Promise. On my honor. I promise.*

She hastily brushed at another tear. *You'd better. Or I'm gonna be mad. And I know people.*

Fierce. His girl was a fighter.

As if he wasn't lost already.

His hands were in her rainbow hair and his mouth on hers before he remembered agreeing to the action.

Guess his wolf was still right beneath his skin.

As Presley relaxed into his body, he let out another growl.

"No sex in the bar," Gee reminded and Paul had the craziest notion to laugh.

He put his forehead to Presley's and she sighed. "Go. Hurry back."

"I'll stay with her, Paul." Saja stood next to them and her soft smile eased a bit of his fear.

He hugged her quickly and then gave Presley one

more kiss because he couldn't not touch her.

Ryker opened the door and went out. Paul followed. One last look at his girl as she stood arm in arm with Saja, and he was out in the crisp sunlight again.

Paul followed the Enforcer willingly but his head wasn't down. Not anymore.

He was proud of what he felt for Presley and he wouldn't cower any longer.

They stopped at the gardens, which seemed an odd place for Ryker to choose to beat the shit out of him. He pulled his notepad and pen out of his back pocket so he could write to him. *Ready to take my punishment.*

Ryker shrugged. "No punishment."

Wrote more. *I lost it in front of her. Shifted. I broke our biggest rule. Secrecy.*

"Shit happens." Had the Enforcer seriously just said that?

Uhh....

He lifted the pad again but had nothing to write.

"You think finding our mate is easy for any of

us?"

Paul hesitated and then wrote, *Maybe.*

Ryker shook his head. "It's not. I brought Saja here when she was stranded in the snow. She was a human. I should have left her alone, but she would have died. I broke every rule of the pack to bring her home. To keep her. Mating is messy. For all of us."

What do I need to do to keep her? To talk to her and answer her questions? Paul turned the pad around to Ryker and he read it.

"A blood oath. To me and to the pack. She will become your responsibility. Her secrecy will be yours to ensure or I'll have to step in to fix the situation. You understand?" He raised an eyebrow. Paul had no doubt what lengths the wolf would go to in protecting the pack and his mate and the child that grew inside her—the winter had taught them all even Ryker had his limits. More, they'd learned he had a heart.

Paul nodded.

"The blood oath we would take will ensure you can keep her. Mate her. This kind of oath comes with a huge responsibility."

65

Paul mouthed the word mate as in a question. Could he really have found his mate? Seemed hard to process even with what he knew he felt for her.

"Yep. Pins and needles when you're touched. Need to take her through the damn roof. Want to bite her. Mount her. Sound familiar?" Had the Enforcer ever said so many words to him? To anyone? Ever? Yet, even amongst the sternness in his gaze—a hint of kindness lurked.

All he could do was nod.

"Not to mention all the fuck-off scent you're putting out." Despite the understanding in Ryker's tone, he lost none of his firmness. "However, she knows nothing of us. She has no idea what she'd be signing up for. This life. This commitment. Humans are different than us. Expectations are so skewed between the species. She can't know anything of us until you swear to protect her and us. And no one can talk to her, including Saja, which she says is killing her." Humor populated his voice at the last. "Better figure it out quick or we're going to have to get her out of town. And you know the rules. No oath. No details. As in none. Got it?"

Hands down the most he'd ever heard Ryker say at one time—ever.

Nodding, he shoved his pad and pen in a pocket and grabbed a knife from the sheath he always wore at his ankle. The same knife had changed his life so many years before. Drew had found it after he won the Alpha challenge and given it to Paul to do with as he chose.

He stared at the blade, gripping it tightly as he opened his hand.

This time. This cut was his choice. One he'd be thankful for, for the rest of his life.

Bringing it down at an angle, he sliced his palm, holding it out to Ryker as blood dripped on the ground between them.

"No hesitation. No need to think. You sure?"

Never more sure of anything in my entire life. Nodding yes, he waited.

"Even if she chooses not to stay? Even if it's a no go on the mating when she knows everything?"

Nodded again. No question.

Ryker morphed one hand into that of his wolf and sliced his own palm. Palm to palm, they completed the blood oath and something passed between the men. Something Paul never expected to experience.

A kinship he'd thought lost forever.

With one last squeeze, Ryker let his hand go. "Can I ask a question?"

Paul raised his eyebrows in question as he sheathed the blade and stood again.

Ryker looked at his ankle then back up. "Same knife?"

He didn't have to elaborate.

A single nod.

"You didn't get rid of it after Drew gave it to you." Not a question.

He took out his pad and wrote, "I couldn't let it beat me."

Ryker nodded. "Your choice this time?"

Mine, he mouthed.

Staring at him, Ryker continued. "You had the ability to tell her anything last night. Or everything.

You didn't do it."

Pen to pad. "I would never betray this pack. Never." In a single moment, he knew his oath to be true.

They stood there, something else passing between them as Ryker smiled. Something else Paul never expected to feel again. Especially not from the wolf standing before him.

Respect.

As he turned to leave, Ryker stopped him. "Paul?"

Paul turned around.

Waited as Ryker lifted his left hand and signed, *Welcome home.*

Stunned, Paul couldn't think past his heart thudding in his chest.

He thought of writing him a message, and looked at the pad and paper in his hand he'd relied on for so long. It had been a method to communicate but it had also been a weapon. A shield to keep him separate from the rest of the members of the pack.

He didn't want to talk to him from behind the

barrier anymore. Not any of them. So he tucked the pad and pen back in his pocket, and signed back. *Thank you, brother.*

Walking away, he blew out a breath. He'd always wondered what it would feel like to be able to speak to his pack again.

To his family again.

The answer?

Perfect.

Chapter Five

Paul had been gone a while and more people filed into the bar for lunch. PG was a nervous wreck hoping each person was him and they weren't.

"He'll be fine," Saja repeated for the millionth time.

"You have nothing to back it up with. Right, right, right. You do, but you can't tell me anything. Got it." The door opened again and she held her breath then, when it wasn't him, she deflated. Again. "Why can't you tell me anything again? I know the answer but seriously I need you to fill the void so I don't lose my shit."

Saja took her hand across the table and pulled her closer with an understanding smile. "Some secrets aren't mine to share. Some secrets are so special people have given their lives to protect them. And some have fought death itself to be here today to keep the same secrets."

PG squeezed her hand and urged her to continue.

"There must be something you can tell me. Anything," she whispered, not knowing how much more waiting she could take, especially after the no sleep she'd pulled the night before as she paced the floors upstairs in her temporary room.

"I have a feeling you're not going to have to wait much longer."

"How do you know? It could be hours still. Your man did not look pleased when he left with—Paul." Wanting to say *her man* didn't make it true, especially since he'd left her in the bar with nothing but a couple kisses to tide her over. And after what she saw him do the night before, she needed a whole lot more of the *chitty chat* to assuage the, *that's not humanly possible,* she'd come up with in the last lonely twelve hours.

"And there he is now."

PG looked over her shoulder at the door which was totally closed. "No he isn't. There's nobody…there."

The door opened and there he stood, backlit by the sunshine, smiling.

She squinted because it was so bright and her eyes watered.

Yeah.

The sunshine. Totally the reason her eyes were moist. Again.

Out of her seat before he even let the door shut behind him, she peppered him with questions one after another as he walked closer. Everyone else in the bar openly watching them made no difference to her. "What's going on? What's happening? Are you in trouble? Where'd you go? Oh my gawd, is your hand bleeding?"

Then he was there, kissing her, touching her, holding her, and breathing her in.

And her brain went quiet. All thoughts and anxiety disappeared. All her worry of the last day and the last hour vanished as his taste hit her system.

No idea how long they stood there. She was pretty certain there was a catcall or two at some point, but she didn't care. The man holding her possessed her complete attention.

The strain of his back beneath her fingertips as he

pulled her tightly against him tugged a sigh from between her lips. "I thought for a little while there I'd never see you again." She spoke to his chest but then looked up into his eyes. "Why can't you talk to me?"

He raised his hands to sign to her.

"Wait. You are bleeding." She grabbed a couple napkins and dipped them in her water then proceeded to clean his palm. For all the blood on it, she expected quite a cut, but when she got it all wiped away nothing was there except a dark-pink line. "You were bleeding." She said it out loud but it honestly wasn't meant for anyone else to hear.

Pulling his hand back, he signed. *I cut my hand.*

"Clearly." She folded the napkins up and tossed them on the table and scowled at—everything.

No. I cut my hand.

Why would you willingly cut your hand?

Because I had to take an oath. A blood oath.

An oath to whom?

Ryker.

Okay, but why? she asked with a whole lotta silent attitude.

74

So I could talk to you. Answer your questions. Explain what happened. What I am. He looked around the bar. *What we are.*

PG looked at Saja who gave her two thumbs up.

This is a big deal, isn't it?

He nodded. *A very big deal.*

So many questions ran through her head she had a hard time focusing on one to ask. She settled on a broad one. *And you can talk to me now because of the oath you gave Ryker?*

Yes.

Are you the only one who can talk to me? The only one who can share with me?

He shook his head. *Ask Saja something.*

PG faced her friend. "Are you a wolf, too?"

Saja looked at Paul and he held up the hand he'd cut. "Finally. No, I'm not."

"Is Ryker a shifter like Paul?"

"Yes. He's a shifter. Slightly different kind than Paul, but, yes, he's a wolf when he wants to be."

"Are you going to have a puppy?"

Saja laughed. Hard. "No." She laughed some

75

more. "If we're lucky, he or she will be a shifter, too, when they get old enough."

"Are you happy? Safe?" It wasn't what she'd meant to ask, but it seemed vitally important.

"Never been happier or more protected in my entire life. These men and women. This pack. It's exactly where I was meant to be. Who I was meant to help. And I have a feeling you and I might have a similar destiny."

"Fate."

Saja nodded and got up from the table. Stepping close, she wrapped her arms around her and held on tight for a second and then spoke to her. "Remember two things for me. Keep an open mind no matter what you hear, and we could really use someone like you and your particular talents."

"What? A grant proposal writer and a kinky people person."

"'Exactly!" She hugged her again and looked at Paul. "Is he still at the garden?"

He nodded and then signed to PG. *Will you tell her yes, and have her thank him for me? For everything?*

"He said yes, and wants you to thank Ryker for everything."

Saja leaned up and kissed him on the cheek. "I'd be happy to. And it goes without saying not to hurt her or I'll come after you with all of my hormonal crazy, right?"

He pulled PG next to his side and nodded.

"Good." She faced PG again. "Call me when you come up for air and you have questions your mate can't answer about girlie stuff. Bye." And with such an open-ended parting comment, she was out the door—two of the men stationed at a table near the door stood and followed her. Everyone else in the bar was enjoying their Gee diet and her uncertainty.

"She said mate."

Paul stayed still for a second. *Yes, she did.*

What did she mean by mate?

He hesitated, and then closed his eyes and signed to her. *Two people meant to be together. Fated to be together even. A pairing so intense and amazing there is a physical, mental, and emotional connection holding them together.*

And you think I'm your mate?

He nodded.

Why do you think so?

The connection. He touched her cheek and pleasure raced to her pussy. Her clit.

The need. He pulled her close and a whimper slipped out of her as he brushed his erection against her. *I've never had that before. Not ever.*

The need for him skyrocketed to some kind of level she didn't know existed.

She wasn't a casual sex person. She could take care of herself if she needed to get off, so fucking for the sake of having a live dildo had never done anything for her.

Being on birth control was to regulate her and nothing more. Had nothing to do with the actual sex component, except for now and with the man standing in front of her. Her head coughed up another *now* as his nostrils flared.

His growl rumbled through her.

It shouldn't have been sexy. It should have been

territorial and archaic and made her feminism stand up and take notice.

Instead she melted against him and wanted to drown in the pools of lust in his blue eyes.

The promise, he signed to her.

What promise?

The oath. It's a promise. A promise for you to keep us a secret.

Paul, I didn't make a promise.

No. I did.

Which makes no sense. If I don't keep my promise, then nothing would happen to me. Something would happen to.... The far-reaching implications of his promise hit her broadside. "Your oath makes you responsible for me and my secrecy." Her hands were shaking so bad she couldn't sign. That hadn't ever happened before.

Mates. We protect each other. He started to sign something but stopped when someone bumped into her.

"Sorry. Whoa, Paul, seriously. It was an accident." The man who'd come in with Tasha the night before backed up a step.

In less than a heartbeat, Paul had moved her behind him and bared his teeth to the unlucky guy who'd accidentally bumped into her trying to get to a table.

"Paul, let's go outside. Take a walk. You can show me around since we got interrupted last night. Paul?"

"Paul." Gee walked up and since her man still hadn't moved out of some kind of attack position, he took Paul by the back of the neck and shook him once. Hard. "No bloodshed in the bar." One more shake.

One more snarl.

"You hear me?"

Paul blinked and with a shake of his head he really looked at Gee.

"Go." He released his neck and squeezed his shoulder with a glance at PG and a wink. Back to Paul, he nodded. "You've earned it."

Didn't take Paul two seconds to hightail it out of there with her hand firmly held in his. Past lots of people…err…wolves staring at them, and they didn't dawdle. For once, all of the attention, with her hand firmly held by Paul, she loved it.

Down Main Street, around a corner then down another street until he led her into a house and closed the door.

Nerves and excitement warred inside her.

The house wasn't huge. She'd been in enough structures in her life around the US to know this house was fairly new, built by hand, clean.

"You built it." She made it a statement. He waited for her opinion. And she could tell it was important to him, which made her love it even more.

He shrugged.

"Talk to me."

Talk to you….

He looked at her face. Every curve, every facet, and she bit her lip at his attention.

That concept is overwhelming. He looked around his house, touched the back of the couch, turned on a light on one of the simple end tables.

You're the first person I've truly been able to talk

to since I was twelve.

Twelve? She signed back, unwilling to break the intimacy of their silent communication.

He nodded once and put his boot up on the coffee table. He pulled up one pant leg, revealing a knife sheath strapped to his ankle.

The blade was long. Twelve inches from tip to handle. He loosened the leather ties and removed the entire case and then put it up on the mantle. Running his fingers down the set, he was silent for a few moments, and she didn't want to rush him.

The reason he couldn't talk seemed much more sinister now. Harsh. Horrible. An accident, she'd been told. What kind of accident took a twelve-year-old's tongue?

From the look on his face, she knew the story she'd been told wasn't at all the truth.

Paul faced her and motioned around the room. *This was my parents' house. They moved on when the last Alpha was still here. I stayed.*

Alone? You stayed here alone?

Yes.

How old were you?

Sixteen, I think.

Young to be on your own.

I grew up years before that.

PG paused, weighing her words. *When you were twelve? Is that when you grew up?*

One day too late.

What happened a day earlier?

I was naive. A kid with childhood ideas of right and wrong, and I had no instincts when it came to hate and fear.

Who?

Paul's eyebrows dipped low. *Who, what?*

Who stripped your trust from you? Who stole your childhood at the tender age of twelve?

A man named, Magnum. The Alpha of our pack.

"The Alpha?" She blurted it out, unable to process the info fast enough. *I thought the Alpha in a pack was supposed to be the leader. The protector of everyone. Was I wrong?*

No. That's right. And I thought I was helping. The pack was hungry and I found extra food and I

83

went to the Alpha, thinking I was going to be a hero. He looked at the knife on the mantle and chills shivered up PG's back. *I wasn't a hero. I was an example. He made me a lesson to the pack for speaking up against him.*

She had questions to ask but she honestly couldn't get her hands to work, so she waited until he faced her again.

The food was his secret stash so no matter how bad the winter got, he'd survive. He and his friends who worshiped the ground he walked on. The pack meant nothing to him but blind allegiance and power.

"And the knife?" she asked in a hushed whisper.

He laid his fingers against his lips and brushed them back and forth absentmindedly. He didn't answer her question but he didn't have to.

"What an asshole!" she blurted out and started to pace. "Your Alpha hurt you? That's—that's— horrible. Where is he now? You tell me where he's at and I'll go show him what Southern girls can do with a knife."

He caught her shoulders mid-pace. *Six feet under.*

Drew killed him a little over a year ago when he came back from being exiled. He killed Magnum, his father, to take over the pack. To save the pack.

"So…." PG shivered from where Paul had ahold of her shoulders still. Attraction tried to overcome the hurt she felt for him and she tried to focus. "Drew. He's the Alpha now."

A nod.

"Makes sense. How people acted around him. Why he thought he could tell me I was staying without asking."

Paul tugged her over to the couch, pulling her down onto his lap.

No tongue at all? She went back to signing. Vocalizing what he'd been through seemed so harsh in the light of day.

Not much. Angling his head toward the light, he paused for a second and looked at her.

I'll never judge you. Never think less of you for what you went through. You don't have to show me anything. Not ever, if you're not okay with it. She put her hand over his and squeezed, meaning every word of what she'd said.

He slowly opened his mouth.

There was a short stub at the back of his mouth, one side longer than the other, but that was it. She wanted to cry, to scream, to dig Magnum back up and kill him again.

Instead she stayed strong and seated with the incredible man sharing his life with her. *How hard is it to eat?*

Rough. Chewing not real possible. Blender is my friend. I can still swallow, thank God, or I'd have been dead long ago. Doesn't really matter on taste of what I eat. Well, drink. 'Cause I have no taste buds.

None? she asked with sadness filling her heart.

Bitter is all that's on the back, which is actually pretty gross if you can imagine. A few sour taste buds on the side. That's it.

She touched his face, his brow, his lips. *Why didn't you move on with your parents?*

Shrugging again, he considered her question. *Anyplace else we went wouldn't be home. Wouldn't be pack even though they didn't ever really feel like mine after that day. The Alpha was awful along with his band of assholes, but there were still some amazing people here. And, honestly, I couldn't stand the constant hurt coming off my parents when they saw me. Not anymore. For four years, it nearly suffocated me. Their hurt. Their feelings of being responsible and failing me.*

Isn't a parent supposed to feel like a failure after they don't protect their child?

I guess so. And I have no idea what I would have done in their shoes. From the look on his face it would be much different from what his parents did. *Seeing it every day, they had no idea what to do to help me. So when they chose to move, I decided a clean break would be the best for both of us.*

Definitely an adult decision, with adult consequences, but along with childlike feelings and repercussions she was sure. How awful. She rubbed his hand with the pad of her thumb and had no clue if she was soothing him or herself.

The new Alpha, Drew, he's better. Amazingly better. Cares about bringing the pack back together.

Rebuilding the town. Growing together. Protecting each other. Evolving with the world around us. He looked around the living room. *So I stayed. Fixed up the house after Drew took over. Rebuilt a lot of what was so horrible. It's safe and I'm proud of it.*

Proud is probably the understatement of the year of what I'd feel, accomplishing all you've overcome. It's beautiful. And we need to have a huge conversation about everything, but all I can think about is getting you naked.

I can scent a lie. As if he was challenging her, his eyebrows lowered.

"Honestly?"

He nodded.

Exposing her throat to him, awareness raced up her spine. He let out a bit of a growl. Probably had something to do with the way she moved against the erection she'd been sitting on since he'd pulled her onto his lap. "Ready for my lie detector test."

He sniffed and his dick throbbed beneath her.

Fuck, he mouthed. *I can smell you.*

Which totally didn't turn her off. Another

question popped into her head, and she asked it before she could think better of it. *Have you ever done this before?*

He made an awful face and shook his head. *Is it so obvious?*

She tucked her hair behind her ear and stared at his perfect lips. *Actually, the thought of being your first does it for me. A lot. I'm—surprised you haven't.*

Why? The look on his face told her he couldn't imagine any reason.

You're ridiculously attractive. And if the pack cleared out like you said it did, I can't imagine a dominant wolf like you—

I'm no dominant wolf.

Cue awkward silence. "Huh?" That's all her head could cough up for her.

I'm not dominant. There's the Alpha. Then dominant wolves, like Ryker and Colt, Tasha's mate. Then there are the betas. The females of the pack. Betty, Tasha, Tala. Then there are omegas.

What's an omega? From the look on his face, saying the word kicked up some of those bitter taste buds he still possessed.

Healers, helpers. The non-dominants who are weaker and can take on the jobs beneath the dominants. I'm told we're an important part of the pack. Yet we're below the betas in rank.

You don't sound like an omega.

There was his shrug. He had more in common with Ryker than he realized. *If the shoe fits.*

Huh? You do realize you growled at like half your pack on the way over here, right?

He shook his head and moved his torso away to get a better look at her.

"Sniff me again if you think I'm lying." She moved her hair out of the way, and he didn't hesitate to inhale her scent up the column of her throat.

Then he nuzzled her throat and she dug her fingernails into—his leg. She relaxed her hand and tried to breathe. He needed to hear this. "And your wolf is big."

So. I'm no one.

I don't accept it.

Truth is truth whether you believe it or not.

Well wasn't he more accurate than she could have stated so simply.

"Tasha's accident." Yes, she made air quotes because she had a feeling Magnum cut a much bigger swath through the pack than one true-hearted young boy. "Is she *less than* because of what Magnum did to her?"

Of course not.

She raised an eyebrow at him.

Yeah, yeah. I walked into that one.

"You say an omega is weaker. Are you weaker because you can't talk? Of course not. Your being a survivor doesn't make you weaker. It makes you a rock star." She spoke the words and signed them. They were important and he needed to hear her on every level.

It doesn't make me awesome. It makes me defective and in a gene pool all on my own since wolves aren't born with defects of any kind. So being different isn't a good thing. I will never be able to hold my own with the other wolves. I'm physically weaker because I can't eat like the rest of the pack does. I'd like my steak in a blender isn't actually common. I know you're shocked.

It does, too, make you awesome. First off, you survived the attack, which I'm still not certain how.

It's a wolf thing. We heal faster, live longer, can survive a lot more than a human can. Probably the only reason I survived.

Second, you have a great heart, and you never gave up hope. Which is amazing. And, third, the dietary stuff we can totally help. The supplements out there have come a long way. That will help you some. Plus, you're important to this pack. I've been here how many days and I can already tell you're important here. Being an omega to your pack sounds like an honor.

I'm a waiter.

You help feed the pack, which you've apparently been trying to do most of your life. I'd say that's very important. And help keep the peace if things get out of hand at the bar, I'm sure.

So I don't have to clean up the mess.

You hear things.

Because I'm invisible.

Laying her palm on his cheek, she stared into his eyes. "I saw you."

Closing his eyes, he leaned into her touch. *Yes, you did.* Leaning forward and pulling her to him, he kissed her.

She pushed away. "Plus, you can't eat the food, so it's a perfect job for you to stay fit and sexy." She bobbed her eyebrows at him, smiled, and kissed him again. And again until they sighed. "You can be anything. You help your pack. And what's to say you can't be an omega to the pack and a dominant in other ways. People, and wolves apparently, live so rarely in only one color of the rainbow."

He touched her hair.

"If what you're doing isn't enough to make you happy, then you find something else that does."

I found you.

"And I make you happy?" She didn't realize how important his answer was until he didn't respond for a minute. She stopped breathing and waited.

I lost my happy a long time ago. Didn't think

anyone could help me find it again.

Which brought her to another question she wanted to ask him. *You've obviously been learning sign language for a while. Like years, for how you sign. Why have you never signed with anyone else here?*

Who would want to learn all of this to talk to me? Only me? Get real.

Apparently, quite a few, since I've already been approached by several members of your pack who'd like to learn if I choose to stay.

Who?

Saja and her man—err—wolf. Going to take some getting used to. *He's already asked me to teach him a few simple things. Home. Welcome. Pack. Brother. Then there's Drew, Tasha, Gee. How many more would you like?*

Gee? The bear?

No, the Wolf. Hold on, what? He's not a wolf?

No. He's a bear.

She shook her head. *And why's he here in the middle of wolf country?*

Long story which no one really knows the whole answer of why.

And Drew. He's your Alpha.

Yes. Hold on a second. I can't think past your list of wolves. Wolves I respect want to be able to talk to me? Really talk to me?

She smoothed his wrinkled brow. "Keeping your pack at arm's length has kept you separate for too long. I think it's time you find your voice."

His hesitancy made it look like it was going to be really hard for him to buy something she saw so clearly.

Looks as if a bit of show-and-tell is in order. We're going to play a game. A kinky game. And I bet we'll have some answers by the end of the game. She stood and pulled him up with her. "Ready to meet your match, wolf?"

A single eyebrow went up. And stayed there as she pulled her shirt up and off.

Then she toed off her shoes. His mouth went a little slack, and she knew she had his undivided attention.

It was nothing like how she normally acted, but life was short and she of all people knew that you couldn't look a gift horse in the mouth.

Gift wolf?

Whatever.

She stripped the rest of her clothes off until she stood before him completely nude.

He took a step toward her but she held her palm out, halting his progress with a touch against his chest.

On your knees, she signed.

He narrowed his eyes at her.

She smiled and eyed the floor between them.

Excitement zipped along her limbs as his upper lip trembled and a tiny growl rumbled out of him.

Staring at him, she bit the inside of her cheek and held his gaze. She couldn't wait to play.

Chapter Six

For a kinky sex game, on the fly, it had some real potential.

One naked cagey wolf and a roll of toilet paper he'd gotten for her out of the closet and set on the coffee table.

Simple. Yet so complex.

The rules are easy. You're going to get naked and I'm going to help. Then I'm going to take this trusty roll of toilet paper and I'm going to wrap parts of your body to the beam in the middle of the open space behind you.

And then? he asked as he clenched his fists over and over again.

She approached him and ran a hand down is chest and then his waist as she circled him. "Then I'm going to suck your cock."

He cleared his throat as her nails trailed down his spine, and he waited for her to come around to the front again. *Doesn't really sound like a game.*

"Sure it is. You're going to be on your knees unable to move."

I can move a lot. It's toilet paper.

"That's the game. If you break the toilet paper, then I stop sucking. See how fun?"

His eyes narrowed and she blinked up at him so innocently and smiled.

"So—ready to play?"

He nodded.

She continued to touch him but dropped the flirtatious vibe for a second. "One serious question. Is your wolf under control? I don't know much about wolves but I can only assume if you shift in the middle of us getting it on, then things could get a bit—tense."

Honestly, I don't know. He paused for a second, closed his eyes, and seemed to listen to something she most definitely couldn't hear. *Pretty sure he is, but you call to him like no one ever has. It's almost like you woke him up.*

You seemed kind of stunned last night when you shifted. It didn't look at all planned.

He shook his head. *I honestly don't know who was more shocked by it. You or me? I've never been moon dependent. Not ever. I've always been able to control it. But from the first time I laid eyes on you, truly looked at you, it's as if my wolf's right beneath my skin. Like we both sensed what you were to us and we both want to get to you. The moon's not out right now so I'm 99 percent certain we're safe.*

"Then we'll do this together and you can stop me at any point. You have the power in the game. Got it?"

He nodded and eyed her naked flesh. She groaned when his fingers skimmed the side of one of her breasts.

Her fingers beneath his shirt on his bare skin ignited an idea inside her. Lifting his shirt, she decided to start the game a bit early. With words.

"My research. What I studied for so long was woven into the BDSM lifestyle."

They both removed his shirt. Him tugging from the top and her pushing the fabric up and out of the way.

Doing it together made her bite her lip. It was special. And she knew it.

He lifted her chin, forcing her to look up, and she almost growled at him. She wanted to see him, explore him, pleasure him.

K. I. N. K? he spelled.

"Exactly." Leaning forward she licked his chest simply to hear him suck in a sharp breath. Trying to keep her head in the game instead of throwing her plan out the window, she focused on making sure Paul never again questioned who he was or what he could be if he chose to be. "My master's thesis was about the physiological and psychological responses of both dominant and submissive people. So, people on the top side of things giving the orders, and the people on the bottom side of things following the orders. Everything I did was based on a complete gender neutral study. So I worked with dominant males and females and submissive males and females, along with some trannies and gender reassigned people, too." She backed him up until he leaned against the beam in the center of the room.

His gaze narrowed on her as she moved him, but, to his credit, he didn't balk or dig his heels in. "I was fascinated over and over again how many gender lines blurred in relation to kink."

Looking up into his eyes she lowered herself to her knees before him. One knee and then the next and slowly began loosening his belt.

With rapt attention, he followed her hands, her mouth, her breasts. Never took his eyes from her as she inhaled and exhaled against his abdomen.

Releasing his belt, she popped the top button on his jeans and slowly slid the zipper down over his erection. But she didn't free him, didn't tug the jeans over his cock and swallow him whole.

No.

She had something to tell him first.

"Grab onto the post behind you and lift a foot." She sat back on her haunches and took the foot he offered and set it lightly over the valley her thighs made where they met. She loosened the shoelace and released the tension on the leather and pulled it free then pulled his sock off as well. Stuffing the sock into his boot, she set it aside and moved his foot back. "Next," she somewhat requested with a tap of her fingers on the other boot and a few bats of her lashes.

"Which do you identify with?"

As she loosened the second boot, he leaned against the pole so he could talk to her. *Identify with what? Male or female?*

"No, dominant or submissive?"

Not dominant.

She removed his second boot and put his sock inside, pairing it up with the first, and then moved his foot back. "So submissive?"

His upper lip curled and a grumble disturbed the air around them. Could be her line of questioning or could have something to do with her naked tatas swaying from side to side as she knelt before him again.

The head of his cock had made its way to the opening of his jeans she'd created earlier. Slowly, she grasped the opening and tugged his pants down to reveal something which made her mouth water and her pussy weep for relief.

She didn't know who actually got the pants off, but in short order they were folded and sitting on top of his boots and he was back standing before her, his hands tense beside his thighs.

Her palms rested on his flank and her breath whispered across the flesh of his cock as it bobbed before her as he took several tense breaths.

"I'm still waiting for an answer. So do you identify as a dominant or a submissive male?" She looked up at him. His jaw flexed as he locked his molars together. "I really want to lick you, Paul, but I need to know what kind of consent I need from you before we continue."

Not dominant so I guess you leave me with only one choice.

"Which is?"

Submissive.

"Good boy." Scoring him with her nails down his thighs, she blew across the engorged flesh of his cock and balls and then stood. "Now. I need you on your knees. Then back up against the pole, feet around it. Good. So consent." PG grabbed her trusty toilet paper and Paul watched her. "Do I have your consent to tie you up and then lick, nibble, and suck on your cock?"

Fuck.

"No that will actually come later."

That's what she said.

PG laughed and leaned down to kiss Paul's lips. "So. What do you think? Gonna trust me?" She smoothed his hair forward across his scalp and waited.

Yes I am. I consent but I have a question.

"Anything."

Will you leave my hands free so I can talk to you?

"Absolutely. I love you talking to me. Makes me feel incredibly special to be your first."

Only.

No hesitation at all. He laid it out there.

She'd always thought the idea of being with only one person was limiting and wasteful when there were so many other options out there and a lifetime to sample the world.

If there was a lifetime of the look Paul was

giving her and the way it made her feel inside, then she'd admit to the world she was wrong.

PG had no idea how she got so lucky to be picked for the man on his knees before her, but she was determined to make quite a lasting impression.

She set to work with her roll of double-ply. His thighs, his ankles, abdomen, chest, and her crowning bondage was his throat. Slightly elevated, his chin lifted above horizontal would keep him from being able to look down without tearing the paper. And it would also keep him from being able to see what she did to him. How she was going to do it?

When she would be doing it….

Completely pleased with herself, she tossed the empty roll on the floor.

"Not gonna lie. Seeing you bound is totally doing it for me." She walked around him, touching his exposed arms, shoulders, forehead. "How about a kiss?"

Yes. Yes yes yes.

Stepping fully around him, she planted herself directly in front of him and pointed to one of her nipples. "Right here. I'd like a kiss right here." She tapped her nipple, which was already on the way to being hard and leaned forward so he didn't have to strain. His lips were like velvet. Soft. Luxurious. "And the other," she instructed on a sighing breath.

Shifting to the other side, he kissed her breast, her nipple, exhaling on a groan, and she almost came from his one noise alone. He nipped one tight peak with his teeth, and she moaned and stepped back so she didn't blow her plan.

You smell so fucking good.

"Hmm. Which reminds me." She tapped her lips. "If I'm all the way down there, you won't be able to smell me as much as you can right here. Since my pussy is so much closer to your nose." Probably a huge crock since his sense of smell was better than anything she'd ever seen, but she was trying to be so—helpful.

Spreading her legs she ran one of her fingers between the lips of her sex and gathered wetness from her pussy. "I thought you'd like a little reminder while you couldn't see me."

Holding his chin up, she smoothed a line of moisture above his upper lip. Air puffed from between his lips, and his eyes closed as his nostrils flared. His entire body jolted at the contact, and his erection, which she'd completely ignored up to that point, brushed her leg.

And it was wet, dripping from the tip, trying to get to her.

Leaning down, she whispered in his ear as she got on her knees. "Seems we're both wet."

Never happened before, he signed to her as she backed up so she could get on all fours before him.

"Then let me take a closer look. Safety first and all."

His cock was a thing of beauty.

Thick, straight, weeping from the end, and his erection jumped as she ran her nose along the length of him. "Fuck you smell good." Licking only the top of the crown, she got her first hint of him. "Incredible. Your flavor is…." She licked him again, sucking in a true sample. "Fuck…."

Her fingertips touched as she circled him. Slick

with pre-cum, she slid over his flesh. Once, twice.

The power inside him radiated from his groin as he instinctively tried to pump into her fist. He couldn't move much without straining the paper, which totally did it for her.

Pausing, she warned him. "No breaking the paper, my sexy wolf."

He stopped moving at all and she smiled.

Moving her fingers lower, she brushed them across the sensitive flesh of his sac and a low-level growl hummed between them.

His hands, which had been hanging by his side in fists, felt for her and landed on her head. Knowing he wasn't supposed to take control, he was supposed to be taking his cues from her, didn't keep him from grabbing a handful of her hair.

He tightened his grip as she lifted his cock to her lips and circled him with her tongue.

His growl, it intensified, and he either didn't realize he was doing it or couldn't stop it. Either one made her feel like a femme fatale and he only had eyes for her.

Tugging her off his cock, he pulled her up to her knees and haltingly signed to her.

Something akin to, *This is the best blow job of the century—ever.* It was either that or *I'm about to come.* Both close…ish.

She squeezed the base of his cock, halting his orgasm, and tore the toilet paper from around his throat so he could see her. Watch her.

Taking what she doled out had to be agony for him, especially never being with a female before. His need to come had to be off the charts, yet he hadn't. Ready to pounce barely touched the surface of the tension in his body. His eyes locked with hers, and then they traveled down her body. His hands were on her skin, her throat, her breasts, her abdomen. Everything he could reach without breaking the paper.

His sharp inhale told her the moment he saw what she was doing.

"I'm fingering myself, Paul. Stretching myself because you're big and I don't want to get hurt. And do you know what I'm going to do?"

He shook his head rapidly. Maybe he said no, or maybe he was trying to clear his head of the need to take her, to possess her, to own the wolf inside him she could practically see pacing beneath his flesh.

What are you going to do? He watched her hand, and she would have bet he couldn't see anything much other than the movement.

She pulled her hand away and painted another line of wetness beneath his nose.

His deep rumble nearly made her come as she turned around and got on all fours again. Backing up, she grasped his cock with her free hand and circled it around her pussy. "I'm going to fuck myself onto you. Take you, and give us both pleasure as I swallow you. Fuck you're hard."

Scooting back another inch, she tried to relax her muscles, but she wanted him inside her so badly the need was killing her. Biting her lip, her arousal nearly overwhelmed her. "Oh my gawd, Paul. Do you know what I realized? When you come inside me, and I smell like you inside and out then I can teach you all about fucking my ass."

A snarl PG would never forget for the rest of her life lit up the room with energy as Paul broke through all the paper with one lunge.

He took her down onto the rug, knocking her legs wider. Grabbing the base of his cock, he pushed inside her with a roar. His arms shoved beneath her as he used his hold on her to fuck her. To take her.

Just as she knew he would.

She wrapped her feet over the tops of his lower legs and held onto his arms around her chest. Already on the verge of coming as he stretched her more and more on each stroke, she whispered, "There's my mate."

And then he bit her....

Chapter Seven

Mine. Mine. Mine.

Nothing else could penetrate the sense of ownership Paul felt when he finally couldn't fight the needs coursing through his body.

No.

That wasn't right.

Not completely.

How wet Presley was as he buried himself inside her.

How perfect she felt beneath him, taking what he needed to give her.

How tiny she was beneath him. His to protect. To cherish.

How humbling her trust was in him as he filled her again and again as he bit her.

Marked her.

Mated her.

All of her penetrated his fog or created it or enhanced it or shattered it.

Her pussy fluttered around his cock and he growled into her shoulder, unable to stop, unwilling to pause even a moment of the bond expanding between them. All around them, it took shape.

The marks of her fingernails in his forearm would be in his skin, and he couldn't help but thrust harder as a lightning rod of sensation raced down his spine, shooting from the tip of his cock into her spasming sex.

With a yell, he released her shoulder as he came inside her for the first time. Inside his mate. One of the first real sounds he'd made since being silenced by Magnum so many years before.

And he gave it to his mate.

She deserved—everything.

Quick, tight strokes accompanied each jet of cum as she came with him, her muscles twitching as her hips jerked to meet his thrusts.

Her moan.

It was everything he ever imagined it would be.

Bringing her pleasure as he claimed her, dominated her.

Epic.

And then he heard it.

His name.

"Paul...."

Nothing but a murmur on her lips as she came on him.

He bit her shoulder again and came inside her over and over, riding her through her orgasm as she shuddered all around him.

Letting her be in control wasn't something he could accept. At least not for long. He'd thought he could. Thought he was submissive. Thought he could let her take him.

A low rumble started up again at the thought of being on the receiving end of a kink dynamic with her.

"Paul." His girl mumbled his name on the wisp of a smile as her entire body relaxed beneath him.

Hearing his name from her lips as they collapsed to the side filled him with a purpose he never thought he'd be blessed enough to experience.

The world was quiet all around them as they

relaxed against each other, and he continued to touch her to make sure she was real and not a figment of his imagination.

Not purely quiet though.

Silent.

A word he'd come to loath because it was where he was forced to stay. To hide.

She taught him differently in one perfect moment.

Taught him in the quiet they existed. A connection formed so beautiful no words were needed between them.

Emotions, and something so dangerous he'd never let himself feel it before, expanded until it filled the room. The house. The black hills he'd wrapped around himself to feel safe for years.

Hope.

What a gift she bestowed upon him in that moment.

A future with a mate so perfect she was everything he'd ever dreamed of and more. A woman so beautiful with her rainbow hair and smile, she lit the world.

His mate.

Kissing her hair, he raised himself up on one elbow to peer over her beautiful body. Running his fingers off her shoulder and along her arm until they trailed off the backs of her fingers, he vowed then and there to spend the rest of his life honoring her gift.

Gently, he squeezed her hand, gaining her attention.

Her eyelashes fluttered open, and she moved her head to gaze up at him.

She must have seen something in his eyes, his face, his being because she bit her cheek and smiled.

He nodded to his hand still covering hers, and she followed his gaze as he flipped it over and made a fist.

Finger by finger he raised three.

His pinky.

His pointer finger.

His thumb.

Her gasp jolted her back the tiniest fraction closer to his chest and he leaned into her, protecting her, keeping her safe. Always.

Touching his hand, he scented her emotion. Her tears. Her happiness.

"I love you, too." She shook her head and a tear ran along her nose, which she brushed away. "It makes no sense. Not any of this, but it feels like for the first time in my life I'm exactly where I'm supposed to be."

Raising his hand, he made sure she followed it. *Because you are.*

"But where am I?"

He looked around the room and smiled then focused on her again. *Home.*

"Oh, Paul." Tears overflowed as he broke his silence. Her arm lifted until her palm was on the back of his neck, stroking him, loving him. She pulled him down and spoke against his lips. "And so are you, my mate. So are you."

For minutes or hours or millennia, wrapped around each other was where they stayed.

Legs and arms and emotions intertwined together so completely time ceased to exist.

Slowly he realized they were on a rug, and his girl didn't belong on the floor.

Standing, he scooped her up and took her into the bathroom. After letting the water warm, he bathed her. He washed every inch of her, paying special attention to each part of her beautiful body. Memorizing the canvas of perfection would take him years and he'd do anything to earn the privilege.

When the water started growing cool, he dried her off along with her hair and then laid her in his bed.

They made love.

It wasn't sex.

Wasn't fucking, though it got rough several times. He would wear her marks of passion on his back for days. And she would wear his handprints on the fleshy globe of her ass for longer.

The specifics didn't matter.

Making love came in many forms, apparently, and as he came inside her again with her legs wrapped around his waist and her back arched off the mattress, he knew why fate had dealt him the hand he'd always thought was so unfair.

Realizing, for her, he'd do it all again if he knew she would be his reward.

Hours later, as the moon rose, his wolf prowled even closer to the surface. With the light of a single lamp on the nightstand illuminating them, he signed to her. *I couldn't do it.*

Couldn't do what?

Let you be in control earlier. In the living room. It was the sexiest thing I'd ever seen, but I couldn't do it.

She smiled, but said nothing.

You knew what was going to happen?

With a sly grin she admitted, *Was pretty positive.*

How? Especially when I didn't even know myself.

She looked thoughtful for a moment and touched his face, his lips. *I saw you. I didn't see you through the filter of your past or what had been done to you. I was a complete outsider, what was that? Yesterday? You're incredible.* She made a face as if she couldn't imagine everything that had happened. He understood. It didn't seem possible his entire life could have been changed completely, so quickly.

With her hand on his chest she paused for a moment. *I saw you.* She touched his chest again, his lips, his cheek. *The man. The wolf. The mate. There was no doubt in my mind how the game would end, but I needed you to see what I saw.*

I'm not less than in your eyes.

She shook her head. *Sign that one more time.*

I'm not less than—

Grabbing his hands she stopped him from signing anything else. *Exactly. You're not less than. Never were. I know you don't totally believe me, but since my research seemed to be at an end, I have some free time. If you'd like me to stick around so we can chat about it. I've never been free. Ever. It's almost as if it were meant to be.*

He stared at her, smoothing the back of his fingers across her cheek. *Remove almost. You were meant to come here. And I was meant to take care of you. To dote on you. I want you to be happy. Fulfilled. So if it means leaving the hills....* He took a deep breath before continuing, but she could tell he was completely serious. *Then we should go. We can go anywhere you want. As long as I'm with you, I'll be home.*

"You're the most incredible man I've ever met." Staring at him, she wondered if she might be dreaming. "You'd leave your pack? Your home? Everything you've ever known?"

He simply nodded and kissed her mouth. *Some things are worth sacrificing for.* Holding her closer, he kissed her again and seemed so happy simply touching her.

"When I had lunch with Saja, she said she was working on finding people, searching for people who belong here in the hills. Didn't really make a lot of sense. Now it does. She mentioned needing some help. I adore her and we've worked together on things before. I could absolutely talk to her about it. Plus, Drew mentioned wanting help with grants for the Black Hills and I could absolutely rock that out."

She glanced up at him and ran her hand over his close-cropped haircut.

"And people want to learn to sign and I'd be honored getting to help you reconnect with your pack. I love being with people, learning their stories. Family is super important and I've missed having it for a long time. I wasn't ever close to my parents. No siblings. Always wanted a big extended family and I think this is exactly what the pack is."

He looked at her. Staring inside her, seeing something, she didn't know what, but then he signed to her. *I'll be your family. Your mate. Till death. And maybe beyond, because one lifetime isn't going to be enough for me.*

He kissed her, offering himself to her. A lifetime of love was one tiny word away, and she'd waited too long to do anything but leap on the chance of epic kinds of happy.

"Yes." She kissed him, and kissed him again, holding his face in her palms so he couldn't look away. "A family, a lover, a partner. All of it and more."

She went to kiss him again, but he stopped her, looking wary. *One more thing. I'm a waiter. I'm not ever going to be rich or have a higher position in the pack. It's not how things go here.*

"So? I met you because you were a waiter. You do a job to help your family, and think how your job might change with the ability to talk to them. You're who I fell in love with. An omega to your pack, but you've been quite dominant with me. Which I totally love."

You love what?

"Being something special to you. And just because you aren't some nine-foot-tall behemoth carting around more muscle than a football team, doesn't mean I don't cream at the thought of you between my thighs. You're giving me something no one else gets. How incredible."

Yes you are.

He smiled and pulled her close, face-to-face as they snuggled down in bed to sleep. They'd been at it for hours.

The thought of what they'd done earlier in the front room, in the shower, in bed.

A growl rumbled through Paul and his eyes went

wolf. *I can smell it when you get turned on. And now you smell like me. Fuck.*

"Do you think your sense of smell is elevated because you can't taste?"

I've actually never thought of it. Might have something to do with it. Never thought of it as a plus before. Ever. Might even be something I might talk to Drew about. He shook his head. *Talk. Fuck.*

"The whole world's been waiting for you, I think. High time you share yourself with the pack. They are lucky to have you. And so am I. Mmm…. When your eyes change like that, it's so sexy." She had no idea her voice could sound so hot. Decadent. Sensual.

You being turned on by me and my wolf makes him want to howl.

An actual howl ripped through the quiet night as he pulled her a bit closer. There was barely enough room between them for him to keep signing to her. She wanted to keep talking, but she wanted to do a different kind of talking.

As she kissed his chest she remembered

something they needed to talk about and something she wanted to tell him. "So am I going to stay here with you, or do I need to tell Gee I need to use his room for a whil—"

Mine. You'll stay with me. I'm not letting you out of my sight. I've waited my whole life for you. I'm never letting you go. Ever.

"I was hoping you were going to say that. Nothing would make me happier. And Gee told me he liked my name."

He raised his eyebrows in question.

"PG. Presley Ginger. Paul's Girl. Never really cared for the nickname any more than my first name. It was a toss-up. This morning, early, when I was down in the bar talking with Gee, he said my name was perfect because he can remember who I belong to." She bit the inside of her cheek and then smiled. "Guess he didn't see any other outcome to this. To us. And I…. I like being yours, Paul. I like it a lot."

Good. Because wolves mate for life.

She giggled. Life and the future and fairy tales lit inside her and she couldn't wait to get started.

Walking her fingers down his chest, she made it almost to his cock before she found herself flipped over, flat on her back, with a growly mate kneeling between her thighs.

I want to lick you. But I can't. And you know what? I've got ten fingers, two lips, teeth, and a very eager cock, and there's no time like the present to get better acquainted with how to pleasure my mate.

He kissed between her breasts, her nipples, down her abdomen, and settled between her thighs as if he were going to be there awhile.

"Paul?"

He looked up at her and waited, staring at her adoringly.

She could definitely get used to that. "I loved tying you up earlier. Loved being in charge for a little bit. Could we do it again sometime? Me pleasuring you until you can't stand it anymore and then you have to take me? Dominate me?"

He nodded and his eyes changed, slits appearing as his fingers momentarily brushed the lips of her pussy. *We can talk about it, my mate. We can talk about anything.*

Life as she knew it would never be the same again. Gasping as his teeth nibbled on her clit, she thanked her lucky stars for uncovering her wolf.

Helping him find his voice was only the beginning.....

Want to keep up with the latest news from the Black Hills Wolves?

Black Hills Conversations

Be sure to sign up for the Black Hills Conversations, a monthly newsletter devoted to the Black Hills Wolves and their authors. Each newsletter also includes a free short read.

http://eepurl.com/bgSP3D